SCRUFFY BEAR
AND THE Six White Mice

For Penny

SCRUFFY BEAR AND THE SIX WHITE MICE
A JONATHAN CAPE BOOK 978 0 224 08394 2

Published in Great Britain by Jonathan Cape,
an imprint of Random House Children's Books
A Random House Group Company

This edition published 2011

1 3 5 7 9 10 8 6 4 2

RANDOM HOUSE CHILDREN'S BOOKS
61–63 Uxbridge Road, London W5 5SA

www.**kids**at**randomhouse**.co.uk
www.**rbooks**.co.uk

Addresses for companies within The Random House Group Limited can be found at: www.randomhouse.co.uk/offices.htm

THE RANDOM HOUSE GROUP Limited Reg. No. 954009

A CIP catalogue record for this book is available from the British Library.

Printed in Singapore

SCRUFFY BEAR
AND THE Six White Mice

Chris Wormell

A Tom Maschler Book

Jonathan Cape • London

A small scruffy bear was out
walking one evening when he
came to a wood.

"What a dark and gloomy place,"
he said to himself, and had just decided
that he would walk around the wood,
instead of going through it, when he
heard a noise. A squeaking noise – like
the sound of frightened little animals.

It was coming from the gloomy wood.

Scruffy Bear set off at once to find out what the matter was, and right in the middle of the wood, caught by the last gleam of the setting sun, he found six white mice.

"Help!" squeaked the mice. "We're lost! And now the night is coming we'll be gobbled up by owls – or foxes – or snakes for certain!"

And just at that moment they all heard the hoot of an owl coming from the treetops above . . .

"Quick!" whispered Scruffy Bear. "Curl up tight
mice, and tuck in your tails!"
    And so the mice curled up tight and carefully
tucked away their little pink tails.

A moment later, silent as a ghost, the owl flew down
and found Scruffy Bear standing beside six fluffy
white balls.

"Hello, Bear!" said the owl. "You haven't seen any mice, have you? I'm sure I heard mice, just a moment ago – and it's about time for my supper!"

"Mice? Oh no, Owl," said Scruffy Bear, shaking his head.
The owl looked down at the six white balls and asked,
"But what are those?"

"Those? Why, those are snowballs," replied Scruffy Bear.
  "Snowballs?"
  "Yes, snowballs. I'm collecting them to save for the winter. It's good to be prepared, don't you think?"
  "Ah," replied the owl, nodding. "Very wise, very wise." And he flew off in search of supper.

"Hurry along, mice, hurry along!" said Scruffy Bear when the owl had gone. And the mice all jumped up and ran along beside him.

But they had not gone far before they heard the bark of a fox up ahead.

"Help!" squealed the frightened mice. "A fox!"

"Quick, curl up again, curl up!" whispered Scruffy Bear. "And do remember to tuck in your tails!"

They did. So when the fox stepped out from the shadows, he found Scruffy Bear standing beside six fluffy balls.

"Hello, Bear," said the fox. "You've not seen any mice, have you? There are mice about here somewhere – I smell them!" He began to lick his lips.

"Mice? Oh no," replied Scruffy Bear. "Only eggs."

"Eggs? But they're furry!"

"They're furry pheasant eggs. I'm gathering them for
the furry pheasant – she lost them, silly bird!"

"Ah . . . " said the fox, looking down at the curious
furry eggs. "But I'm sure I smelled mice." And he stalked
off in search of supper.

"Hurry along, mice, hurry along!" said Scruffy Bear when the fox had gone, and all the mice jumped up and hurried along.

But they had not gone far before they heard the hiss of a slithery snake coming from a thicket just up ahead.

"A snake!" squealed the frightened mice.
  "Quick! Curl up, curl up!" whispered Scruffy Bear.
"And remember those tails!"

The mice curled up once more, and a moment later the snake came slithering out of the thicket.

"Hello, Bear," she hissed. "I'm looking for mice. Are there any mice around here?"

The snake was staring at the furry white balls . . .

"Mice? Oh no," replied Scruffy Bear. "Only apples."
  "Applesss?"

"Yes, apples. I've been picking up windfalls – white moon apples that have fallen down from the white apple trees on the moon. It's been very windy up there, you know."

"Moon applesss?" hissed the snake, looking even more closely at the furry white balls. "But whoever heard of applesss with little pink tailsss like that one?"

One of the mice had forgotten to tuck in its tail!

"Oh dear!" exclaimed Scruffy Bear, quickly picking up the "moon apple". "But that's not a tail – that's a naughty little worm eating my apple!"

"A worm? Yuck!" said the snake in disgust, and she slithered off in search of supper.

It was not until later that the snake thought:
"Moon applesss? That's ridiculousss!"

And the owl thought:
"Snowballs? In the middle
of summer?"

And the fox thought:
"Furry eggs? That's absurd!"

And they all thought . . .

"MICE!"

But by then it was too late, for Scruffy Bear and the six white mice were long gone!